HERGÉ

THE ADVENTURES OF TINTIN

FLIGHT 714

METHUEN CHILDREN'S BOOKS

LONDON

**Translated by Leslie Lonsdale-Cooper
and Michael Turner**

**The TINTIN books are published
in the following countries :**

Argentina :	JUVENTUD ARGENTINA,	Buenos Aires
Australia :	HICKS, SMITH & SONS,	Sydney
Belgium :	CASTERMAN,	Tournai
Brazil :	DISTRIBUIDORA RECORD,	Rio de Janeiro
Canada :	METHUEN,	Toronto
Denmark :	CARLSEN/IF,	Copenhagen
Egypt :	DAR AL MAAREF,	Cairo
Finland :	OTAVA,	Helsinki
France :	CASTERMAN,	Paris
Germany :	CARLSEN VERLAG,	Reinbek-Hamburg
Great Britain :	METHUEN,	London
Greece :	PEGASUS,	Athens
Iceland :	FJÖLVI,	Reykjavik
Indonesia :	INDIRA,	Djakarta
Iran :	PAT MARTY,	Teheran
Israel :	MIZRAHI,	Tel Aviv
Italy :	GANDUS,	Genoa
Japan :	SHUFUNOTOMO,	Tokyo
Mexico :	MARIN,	Mexico
Netherlands :	CASTERMAN,	Utrecht
New Zealand :	HICKS, SMITH & SONS,	Wellington
Norway :	SCHIBSTED,	Oslo
Peru :	DISTR. DE LIBROS DEL PACIFICO,	Lima
Portugal :	CENTRO DO LIVRO BRASILEIRO,	Lisbon
Singapore :	BOOKS FOR ASIA,	Singapore
South Africa :	HUMAN & ROUSSEAU,	Cape Town
Spain :	JUVENTUD,	Barcelona
Sweden :	CARLSEN/IF,	Stockholm
U.S.A. :	ATLANTIC -LITTLE, BROWN,	Boston

Artwork © 1968 by Éditions Casterman, Paris and Tournai.
Text © 1968 by Methuen & Co Ltd,
11 New Fetter Lane, London EC4P 4EE
First published in Great Britain in 1968
Reprinted 1968, 1971 and 1973
Published as a paperback in 1975
Printed by Casterman S.A., Tournai, Belgium.
ISBN 0 416 77420 2

FLIGHT 714

A Qantas Boeing 707 touches down at Kemajoran airport, Djakarta. Flight 714 from London arrives in Java, last stop before Sydney, Australia...

I keep telling you. We're in Java!... Djakarta!

How very strange. I'd have sworn it was Djakarta.

This IS Djakarta, ten thousand thundering typhoons!

Rangoon? You must be joking.

Blistering barnacles! Djakarta! Djakarta!! DJAKARTA!!! Can't you listen to what I say?

Botany Bay?...Then why didn't you say we'd arrived?

No, Professor, we're not in Australia yet. It's Djakarta.

Yes, I know. But I thought at first it was Djakarta.

Welcome to Java! Transit passengers this way, please...

Transit passengers... that means us.

This is more like it. I'm no skye terrier... I prefer my feet on the ground!

I say, Tintin, what about a little drink?

Good idea. Why not?

There's the bar, look...

Fine!

Hey!... Stop!... Are you trying to make a fool of me?

There! Look! Kemajoran!... Tell me, is this or is this not Djakarta?

KEMAJORAN (DJAKARTA) INTERNATIONAL AIRPORT

Always the same, isn't it? "Poor old Cuthbert, doesn't listen to a word you say... head in the clouds again... always gets the wrong end of the stick". And on and on and on and on and on!

One of these days he'll send me round the bend... Oh, forget it. Let's have a whisky... Whisky? Drinking whisky when some poor devils can't even afford a cup of tea... Like that old chap ...

Look at him, not a penny... Where does he come from? How long since he had a square meal?

Alone in the world... No one to care... Human flotsam, one of life's failures... even catches cold in the tropics.

AAAAAAAAH

TCHOO

My poor fellow, here's your hat.

AAAAH... AAAATH... AAATHA... 'ank you!

Aha, my good deed for the day! No one saw me slip a five-dollar bill into his hat.

① What's this?... Am I dreaming? It can't be... a five-dollar bill!

② Heaven be praised! At last I can buy food!

③ CHOMP CHOMP CHOMP

④ Thank you, thank you, and... OOP... bless you!

Such generosity... such a noble soul... my unknown benefactor!

He quite definitely said Rangoon!

But...

It's perfectly natural, of course. Anyone in my position would have done the same ...

Billions of ...

SKUT!

SKUT!!...Our old friend Skut, the Estonian pilot...What a wonderful surprise!

Captain Haddock!... Tintin! I glad to see you again!

And this is Professor Calculus. I'm sure you've heard about him.

Yes, yes. I proud to meet you Professor.

No, Calculus.

Skut, you Baltic bandit! We haven't seen you since that Red Sea scrimmage. What are you doing here?

I pilot private aeroplane. You know famous tycoon Laszlo Carreidas?...O.K., him my boss.

Laszlo Carreidas? The aircraft manufacturer?"The millionaire who never laughs"?

That him. Carreidas aircraft, Carreidas cloth, Carreidas oil...stores, newspapers, Sani-Cola...all him. We fly to Sydney to International Astronautical Congress.

Well I'm...! That's where we're going. We've been invited to the Congress... guests of honour, you know... the first men on the moon...

Bravo! I thought you go on new adventure...

No, by thunder! Adventures are out... right out, forgood! This is a pleasure trip, an ordinary flight. No fuss, no upsets, no commotion...

WOOAH

Blasted mongrel, skulking down there! Almost broke my neck!...Telex for you, skipper, here's the flight plan.

Oaf!

Thank you. I introduce: Paolo Colombani, co-pilot with me... My friends: Captain Haddock, Professor Calculus, Tintin.

'Morning!

Hi!

Any trouble, Colombani?

No, skipper. Pressure constant, light wind from the south-east, low cloud base...everything O.K.... See you later.

He is new navigator. Regular navigator fall ill on way, in Teheran... Suddenly to hospital ...Colombani fill place.

Not the nicest I've met!

Clod!

Ah, here come my boss. Mr. Carreidas happy to meet first men to land on moon.

"The millionaire who never laughs"... Him?

Still, he must be kind-hearted; he's taken that little emigrant under his wing. Good _____ for him!

Mr. Carreidas, I please introduce my friends to you: Captain Haddock, Professor Calculus, Tintin. They went in rocket and were first men on moon. You remember?...

I...

How d'you do, Mr. Carreidas.

Er... No... Excuse... this Mr. Spalding, secretary of Mr. Carreidas... Here is Mr. Carreidas.

It can't be!

I never shake hands: it is extremely unhygienic... I do vaguely remember some expedition, but the details escape me... As I recall, it didn't affect the stock market.

Hello?...

There seems to be... Allow me...

Presto!

My hat!... You're a trespi... no, I mean... presti.. prestigidi... prestidigita... ta... ta...

TAAAH... AAAH...

HA HA HA

HAHAHA... prestidigitator!

HEE HEE OH HO HO HAAA

I... ha! ha!... I... it's incredible... incredible... ha! ha! It's quite incredible!

Spalding!

Yes, Mr. Carreidas.

You heard, Spalding?

Yes, Mr. Carreidas.

It hasn't happened for years.

As you say, Mr. Carreidas.

This is an occasion!

Yes, Mr. Carreidas.

Drinks, Spalding!

At once, Mr. Carreidas.

Order the usual, eh, Spalding? We mustn't be extravagant, must we?

No, Mr. Carreidas.

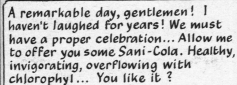

A remarkable day, gentlemen! I haven't laughed for years! We must have a proper celebration... Allow me to offer you some Sani-Cola. Healthy, invigorating, overflowing with chlorophyl... You like it?

I... love it!

So you are en route for the Congress in Sydney. I heard you'd be coming along.

Hong Kong? No, we're attending the Congress in Sydney.

Ha! ha! ha! He's price-less. A natural clown!

Sydney... Sydney? ...I wonder...

Tell me, Captain, as a seafaring man I'm sure you're fond of ba...baa...baa...

Black sheep?

BAAA

...ttleships...Battle-ships... You're an expert?

I...er...I mean, I was in the merchant service. I don't know much about naval warfare. One of my ancestors went in for that sort of thing...

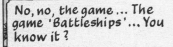

No, no, the game...The game 'Battleships'...You know it?

Well, I have played...yes.

Spalding!

Yes, Mr. Carreidas.

Pay attention.

These gentlemen are travelling with us. Have their airline tickets cancelled and transfer their baggage to my aircraft right away.

But Mr. Carreidas...

But...

But we...

Bombay?

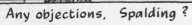

Any objections, Spalding?

No, Mr. Carreidas, I was thinking...

I don't pay you to think, Spalding.

No, Mr. Carreidas.

It's very kind of you, Mr. Carreidas, but we really cannot...

Rubbish!... Your health!

Patience, Spalding, your time will come.

DONG Qantas airlines announce the departure of their flight 714 to Sydney. All passengers to gate No. 3, please.

First I must warn the chief!

But Mr. Carreidas... our baggage ... and our reservations ...

Don't give it a thought. Spalding will arrange everything.

But there's Snowy... he's such a fidgety traveller, and ...

Snowy ... fidgety ... Great snakes!

SNOWY

He's gone! He's escaped from his lead! Look, he's chewed it through and slipped off somewhere. Excuse me... I must go after him!

Now where's that rapscallion?

Meanwhile ...

Is that you, Walter?...Spalding here...Quick...Listen...You must contact the chief: old Sneezewort has invited three people to travel with us... friends of the pilot... met them accidentally. So it's all off... Understand?

Too late, Spalding: everything's fixed. Anyway, you don't really imagine the chief's going to change his plans for three stray hangers-on?...You have your orders; do as you're told.

But Walter, with three extra passengers the whole thing could be wrecked, and if...

So there you are, rascal! Come here!

Nicked! Back on that dratted lead!

Walter, you must listen...

CLICK

I know you hate this but you have to wear it... You'll land me in all sorts of trouble...

?

!

I... I didn't see you there... I was ...er... telephoning...A distant cousin who...er... lives in Djakarta ... Now I must see about your luggage and cancel your reservations...

I'm sorry to be a nuisance...

Not at all. Delighted to be of service.

See you later.

DONG This is the last call for Qantas airlines Flight 714 to Sydney. All passengers please go immediately to gate No. 3.

He was spying on me!

A cousin, indeed! That's a tall story!

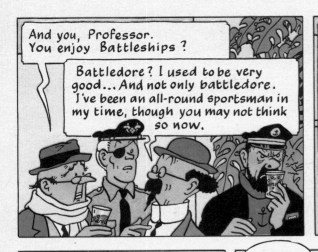
And you, Professor. You enjoy Battleships?

Battledore? I used to be very good... And not only battledore. I've been an all-round sportsman in my time, though you may not think so now.

Tennis, swimming, rugger, soccer, fencing, skating... I did them all in my young days. Not forgetting the ring, too: wrestling, boxing, and even savate...

Savate?...

No, no, no! I said savate, French boxing ...Stars above! They make me laugh nowadays with their judo and their karate. Savate! That was real fighting!...

Using your feet as well as your fists... I was a champion ...unbeatable ...just you watch this...

HUP!

THUMP

Perhaps I'm a little out of practice. It'd soon come back if I went into training.

Isn't it time you stopped acting the goat?

Ha! ha! ha! He's a remarkable fellow!

I beg your...?

Er...I...er... was saying you... must stop tiring yourself out.

Everything is settled, Mr. Carreidas. We can go now.

And about time too, Spalding!

?

Are you coming, Captain?

Yes... straight away.

Spalding was right. Sneezewort has collected three passengers... that's their bad luck! ...But...but...

I must be seeing things! ... It's Tintin!!

This is my newest brain-child: the Carreidas 160. A triple-jet executive aircraft, with a crew of four, and six passengers. At 40,000 feet the cruising speed is Mach 2, or about 1,250 m.p.h. The Rolls-Royce-Turbomeca turbojets deliver in total 18,500 lbs of thrust...

It's magnificent!

WOOAH

The most advanced feature lies in the aerodynamics of the ...

Ah, there's Gino, my steward ... A Neapolitan. I wonder ...

Telefono from New York for il signor Commendatore.

That'll be Goldberg.

Hold the line, please.

Please board the aircraft, gentlemen. Gino, look after my guests.

Si, signor Commendatore.

Hello... Yes... Of course: the Parke-Bennet sale... Well?...Three Picassos, Two Braques and a Renoir ...Junk! ... Anyway, I haven't an inch of space to hang them.

What's that?... Onassis after them? ...Then buy! ... Get them all! ... What?...I don't care how much, buy!

You met navigator Colombani... This is new radio operator, Hans Boehm.

Hello!

Captain!

Well, well ...

More new crew?

Si... no fortuna we have on this viaggio... Other radio operator in accidente at airport in Singapore... with petrol tanker...

But presto presto il signor Spalding find new radio operator...Il Signor Spalding is molto intelligente... Il Signor Spalding ...

THUMP

? ?

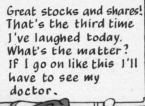

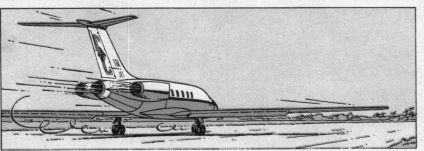

C4 - D4 - E4? Not a bad start, Captain. You've sunk a submarine, but the other two shots went into the water.

Aha!

This is going to be good!... Now for my pipe. Oh, I hope the smoke won't bother you?

Smoking is strictly prohibited, Captain. Even the smell of tobacco upsets me.

!

My turn now. Let me see... A4 - B4... and... er... C2.

Good shot Mr. Carreidas!... A destroyer sunk with two shells, and a hit on another destroyer.

Now I'll have a go. I must fight back! ... C5 - D5 - E5

Bad luck, Captain! All three shots into the sea... I think I'll try A8 - B8 - C8.

Blue blistering barnacles!

A cruiser sunk: three direct hits!... You're psychic!... Still, what do you say to C6 - D6 - E6, eh?

All missed, I'm afraid... What bad luck!... I haven't got second-sight, you know... just natural talent, that's all. Now I must concentrate ...

Anyone'd think he could see my board ... And what's more, he won't let me smoke!

Hello, that's odd ... I'd swear... I must be dreaming ...

For my third salvo : G1 - G2 - G3

THE WING!

The wing? What about the wing?

What about the wing?...Nothing, except it's come loose!

A goose?... Really?... Where?

"It's come loose"! Ha! ha! ha! Oh! ho! ho! AHAHAA!

I beg your pardon, but I don't see what's so amusing about being in an aeroplane that starts shedding it's wings in mid-air!

What a pity! I didn't see the goose... but modern aeroplanes move so fast.

There's no danger to the aircraft, Captain. It's just the swing-wing in operation.

Very funny! "Just the swing-wing". What might that mean?

Well, the wings are pivoted at the leading edge. The pilot has to move them forward to give maximum lift for take-off or landing. As he goes through the sound barrier he has them in mid-position. Then in supersonic flight he swings them right back: and that's what's happening now...

But let's get back to our game. See what you think of my next broadside, Captain. G1-G2-G3.

Ten thousand thundering typhoons! Three direct hits on my battleship! You're incredibly lucky!

Just a matter of skill, Captain. Skill and logic... Your turn.

Now why is Spalding getting so agitated?

He keeps looking at his watch, too ...Very odd!

E1-E2-E3

He's getting up... Why?

All three into the water!

I'll just go along to the pilot's cabin, Mr. Carreidas... to see everything's all right.

Do you have to keep disturbing me, Spalding? Can't you see I'm busy?

It's my turn to fire, Captain.

I don't think I trust our friend Spalding ...

Mr. Carreidas sent me along: he wants to know our position.

We've just passed the radio-beacon at Mataram on the island of Lombok. We're heading now for Sumbawa, Flores and Timor.

Good.

By the way, skipper. Mr. Carreidas would like a word with you.

Me?... Then I'll come at once.

You take over the controls, Colombani.

O.K.

You go. I'll be along.

G-6, H-6, I-6,

The old man cheating again.

Thundering typhoons! still bang on target! It's fantastic!

A cruiser sunk! Holed three times!... Now I'll try...er... F-1, F-2, F-3.

A destroyer hit once, and two shots wide ... Well, what is it?

You send for me, Mr. Carreidas?

Me?... No?... Why?

But Mr. Spalding just come and say to me...

Spalding? That half-witted...

Is it not true, Mr. Spalding, you say...

Hands up! Come on, all of you!

SPALDING!?!

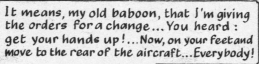

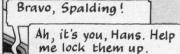

Open the door, Spalding!... Otherwise I'll...er...I'll ...Spalding!

A few more seconds and I'd have fixed him, but you saw...

Spalding is two-faced crook!

Fraud!

Mamma mia!

Are you addressing me?

Now call up the control tower at Macassar. Pitch some yarn or other to keep them quiet.

Spalding!...Spald-i-ing! I didn't mean to be cross!...Now come along, be a good boy, Spalding, open up!

Macassar tower? This is Golf Tango Fox. We are just passing over Sumbawa. Nothing to report. We'll call you again before we reach the Darwin control zone. Over and out.

O.K. Now straight down to sea level.

Going down?... Where shall we be landing?

You ask hi-jackers up front!

My ears are singing like Castafiore in full spate!

Swallow and it goes.

Swallow what?

Swallow, that's what

We still descending. They want to fly low, they escape from radar.

Swallow?

I suppose so.

Swallow?

GLUG

Ah, my ears have popped. She's gone!

We'll soon be in the clear...

Kurang adjar! Apa tidah bissa djaga sajapoenja lajar! Apa gilah!

Macassar tower calling Golf Tango Fox! What has happened? Are you receiving me? We have lost radar contact... Please report your position. Over.

Macassar tower calling Golf Tango Fox! I repeat: we have lost radar contact. Report your position. Golf Tango Fox, are you receiving me? Come in please. Over!

Aha! That's done the trick!

Mamma mia!

Why?

A pleasure trip! Ha! ha! Very funny!

Spalding!

We change course.

Spalding, this is treason! You'll live to regret it, Spalding!... Spalding, you hear me?... Spalding, speak to me, Spalding!

What d'you suppose is behind all this, Mr. Carreidas?

A foreign power, undoubtedly, or a rival company, trying to steal my prototype.

Or perhaps it's just a straight case of kidnapping... to extort a big ransom.

They won't get a penny! Not a penny! Never!

Macassar tower to Darwin tower. We have lost contact with Carreidas 160 Golf Tango Fox, destination Sydney. Last radio contact passing over Sumbawa. Are you in touch with this aircraft please?

They'll soon raise the alarm and ... Ah, there's our radio beacon!

We're home and dry!

Home and dry?... Don't count your chickens, Inglese!... It isn't all over by a long chalk!

Why? ... What do you mean?

(15)

What do I mean?... Just this: the runway we're going to land on is about a quarter the length we need for a bus like this!... So, you can reckon it's ten to one we'll break our silly necks!

There's our rendezvous: the island of Pulay-pulau Bompa.

Right. We'll regain height to 1000 ft, reduce speed, set the wings for landing, empty the tanks. And in we go!

They climb again. I think prepare to land... Yes, there is island ... And there is runway ... But...crazy! Is crazy! Runway much too short!

They're ready for us.

Yes, I saw.

Ah, the wheels are down, they're coming in.

Flaps down, Hans!

Can't you stop rolling us around, you pock-marked pin-headed pirate of a pilot!

They put down flaps.

All sit with back against forward partition, hands behind head!

Now, Colombani boy, it's all or nothing!

Quick, the parachute!

WHAP

WOOOAAAH
Mamma mia!
Hands behind head, Captain!

CRACK

The parachute's burst!
Reverse the engines!

WOO-OW! Thundering typhoons! some people travel for fun!

WOW-OW-OW Brakes!...Brakes! They're full on!

BANG

The nose-wheel's burst! I can't hold her!

We're going too fast! We're done for!

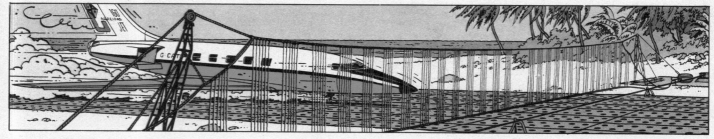

Bashi-bazouks!

Mamma mia!

WOOAAAH

Saved!

Aha! Operation Carreidas successfully accomplished!

Sure!

What a beastly experience! But we're alive, that's all that matters!

We'd better get busy with the prisoners.

Never have I had such a rough landing. You're fired!

Get moving, or I'll be doing the firing! Someone's waiting for you!

WOW-OW-WOO-OW

Keep that animal quiet!

He's absolutely terrified.

Mamma mia!

You wanted me?

Snowy, Snowy, quiet now, Snowy!

WOOAAH

SNOWY!

WOOAAH

Snowy! Here, Snowy! SNOWY!

Fire! Go on, shoot! Kill the tyke. It's gone mad!

WOOAAAH

RRRRR WOOOOAAAAH

RRRRR

RRRRR

RRRR

Murderers! Devils! Let me go! Let me go, I tell you!

Bungling fools! You'd miss an elephant at five yards! Get after that infernal mongrel, and make sure you wipe it out!

That voice!?

RASTAPOPOULOS

Himself, dear boy!

Welcome to my island paradise!

Your surprise is charming to see!... You thought Papa Rastapopoulos was eaten by the Red Sea sharks, eh? Ha! ha! ha! ha!

Now the boot is on the other foot! I have you trapped in my little tropical garden. And you walked in all by yourselves! ... You should have minded your own business, my dear friends, and stayed on Flight 714.

Get rid of that cigar! No one smokes in the presence of Laszlo Carreidas!

Get rid of my cigar? But of course. Your wish is my command, Mr. Carreidas!

We knew you were a swine, Rastapopoulos. Now we know you're a dirty swine at that!

Well said!

Insolent puppy! You dare to defy me? When I have you here in my power?...And I've got you all right, you little fool!

I've got you. I've got you all, and I shall crush you like ... like...

... like I crush an insignificant spider!

Diavolo!

MDJRK

...I...er...you... Anyway, this island will be your grave!

Get everything fixed right away, Allan.

O.K., boss.

You see?

In a couple of hours every trace of you and your plane will have vanished. And your money, Mr. Carreidas, your lovely, lovely loot, will be mine!

You're mad!

It's a bore, you know, to stop being a millionaire... When I went bust, I couldn't face the sweat of making another fortune for myself. So I decided it'd be easier, and quicker, to take yours!

You're mad!

No, just well informed, that's all. I know, for example, that you have on deposit in a Swiss bank - under a false name, of course, you always were a cheat - a quite fantastic sum of money...

I know the name of the bank: I know the name in which you hold the account; I have some magnificent examples of the false signature you use... In fact, the only thing I don't know is the number of the account, and that you are now going to give me!

Never!

Never say "never", my dear Carreidas... Wouldn't you agree with me, Doctor Krollspell?

He! he!

You can torture me! Pull out my nails, roast me over a slow fire...even tickle the soles of my feet... I won't talk!

RRRRRR   RRRRRR

SNOWY!

Ah, getting rid of the dog, I expect.

Cowardly brute!

Hold your tongue! I am talking with my friend Carreidas, not you!

Who mentioned torture, my dear Laszlo? Whatever do you take us for?... Savages?... Shame on you! How vulgar!... We aren't going to hurt you. Kind Doctor Krollspell has just perfected an excellent variety of truth-drug. It's a painless cure for obstinate people who have little secrets to conceal.

A truth-drug?... Villain!... Blackguard! ...Bully! ...A...aa... aaa...

AAAA

TCHOO

Stop! My hat!...

Whoops!

Take him with you, Doctor Krollspell. Get your little black bag ready. I'll join you in a minute.

My hat!... My hat!...

Come along!

Give the poor chap his hat, you son of a sea-gherkin! He could get sunstroke!

My hat!...

Sunstroke, eh? But what about you? You aren't wearing a hat either...

Don't worry about me.

But I do. I want you wrapped up!

Ten thousand ...

Ha! ha!

Ha! ha!

Tramps!...Terrapins!...Two-timing troglodytes!

Enough fooling: take them to the cooler.

O.K.

21

Come on, get going!...The old boozer's had a drop too much. Can't see the end of his nose. Tintin, you're in charge of the steering. Now then, on your way!

He who laughs last laughs longest. Remember that, pockmark!

We're going uphill. Get in single file. Don't forget, Tintin, you're in charge of bluebeard!

Left, Captain...

Right...A little more to the right...That's it...

Now keep to the left...

Straight ahead...

Careful! Keep left now...

GRMBLLL

Left, Captain, left...

LEFT!!

LEFT!!!

RIGHT left, Cap...

DOINNG

Ten thousand thundering typhoons!...Just you wait, Allan! When I get my hands on you I'll stuff your cap right down your throat, badge and all!

Ha! ha! ha!

Come on, keep moving. Not much further.

Will you step into my parlour, gentlemen?

Home sweet home: an old Japanese bunker. And here you stay till Carreidas talks. So make yourselves comfortable.

What happen to us afterwards?

I'm not supposed to tell you yet; boss's orders. But I'd hate to keep a secret from old shipmates like you...You'll go back on board the aeroplane, which will then be towed out to sea...

and sunk. With you inside, of course! ...Ha! ha! ha!

CLANGGG

Scorpion!

Baboon! ... Orangoutang!..

Ha!ha!ha!

Bandit!... Bootlegger!... Bashi-bazouk!... Breathalyser! Brigand!

Keep your hair on, Captain... I mean... Come and let me try to get that hat off!

'ull 'ard, 'a'ain!... 'ull! 'ull!

Can I be of any assistance to you?

'ooray

Billions of blue blistering barnacles, I... Oh, sorry!...

HA! HA! HA! HA! It suits you! You look fabulous!

It's disgraceful!... Yes, disgraceful!... I said disgraceful!

Ssh!... Quiet!...

Why? What's the matter?

I suppose you think it's funny!

No, it's nothing... I thought for a minute I could hear Snowy barking.

Of course. Poor old Snowy!

Disgraceful! That's what I call it!

Don't you worry, Tintin. If we get out of this alive we'll make the butchers pay. I'll...

Thanks, Captain. Whatever we do, it won't bring poor Snowy back to life.

I ...er... well... yes...hm... er...

Anyway, remember our own death sentence is only suspended, until Carreidas talks... But I wonder, will he talk?

He'll talk, Mister Rastapopoulos, he'll talk all right.

I hope so for your sake, doctor!

Never!... And anyway, I want my hat!

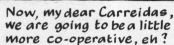

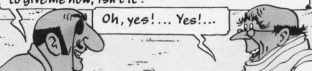

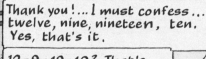

Poor Elena! How she protested her innocence. But they threw her into the street...And I nearly died of laughing! Even then I was the devil incarnate!

The dose can't have been strong enough. I'll give him another shot.

Very well.

I was only a child. From my tenderest years I have never ceased to do my neighbours down. Amazing, isn't it?

Th - ere!

Now who's going to give his account number to his old friend Rasta-popoulos, eh?

Me!...Me!...I am!

2. 17. 6...

2. 17. 6? Excellent my dear Carreidas. That's all I wanted to know.

Yes, 2.17.6. That was it. The exact amount. I sneaked it one morning, some years later, from my elder sister's handbag.

You dare to joke with me?

Believe me, it is no joking matter. I am rotten, rotten to the core.

Your account number! Tell me! I order you to tell me!

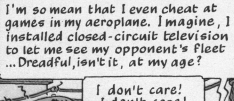

I'm so mean that I even cheat at games in my aeroplane. I magine, I installed closed-circuit television to let me see my opponent's fleet ...Dreadful, isn't it, at my age?

I don't care! I don't care! I don't care!

But you should care. There are lessons to be learned from the life of a dishonest...of a...dishon... dis... ZZZ-ZZZ-ZZZ

He's gone to sleep!... Your serum is a success, Doctor Krollspell! A brilliant success!

Meanwhile...

If we get out of this mess alive I swear I'll never touch whisky again ...

... for a hundred ... no, fifty ... er, say ten... well, three days... That's a promise!

Ssh!...Quiet!...Listen!

I didn't say anything!

It's Snowy!... I'm sure it's Snowy!...Listen!

Nnn! Nnn!

It's Snowy! He's alive!... Snowy!

Ssh! Keep quiet!

Nnn! Nnn!

Quiet, by thunder!... You'll bring the guards in!

Nnn! Nnn!

You hear dog?... I tink...

I hear 'um.

Calm down, Snowy, calm down.

Nnn! Nnn!

Ssh-h-h-h

Nnn! Nnn!

Golly, what's the matter? He's tied up.

Go on, Snowy, Go on!

SCRUNCH SCRUNCH SCRUNCH

He's done it! I can free my hands. Thanks, Snowy!

Wonderful! Three cheers for Snowy.

NO!

HIP HIP !

HOOOOOO ...RAY!?

What's the matter?

Blistering barnacles, what have I done...

Someone's coming...

Which man cry?

Let's hope Snowy understands what to do...

I don't care what anyone says, it's a thoroughly stupid joke!

Which man 'e go cry?... You tell!

He's there... He understood.

OUCH

?

YEOW

Now for it! One, two, three!

WHAM

WHAM!... Well done!

Fine left hook!

WHAM

Fine right uppercut for other one!

And again! Bravo!

First, let's take that hat off poor Calculus.

A neat job, eh, boys?

Ma professore, it was not uno joke.

I don't deny it. It was just a stupid joke, that's all.

Now we must try to rescue poor Mr. Carreidas.

Poor?... Him?... Risk our lives for that cheat?

How'd we find him, anyway, miserable old Midas?

By using his hat.

Using his hat?

Yes. Where is it?... Ah, on the floor.

Get the scent, Snowy.

Sniff, sniff... That reminds me of someone...

Find him, Snowy!

Seek him out!

I... er... it will work this time, Mister Rastapopoulos. I've doubled the dose... I... I shall succeed...

I strongly advise you to, doctor!

ZZZZ

ZZZZ

ZZZZ

You were wearing this hat, Captain. That's why Snowy made a mistake.

Anyway, thanks to Snowy at least we're free, and can look for Mr. Carreidas.

I know, but rescuing him is another matter.

I've got a suggestion. The Captain and I go in search of Carreidas. You, Skut, take the Professor, Gino and the prisoners, and hide somewhere near the bunker. Keep out of sight, and wait till we come back. Is that all right?

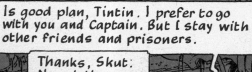

Is good plan, Tintin. I prefer to go with you and Captain. But I stay with other friends and prisoners.

Thanks, Skut: Now, let's go.

Ready, Professor?

Extraordinary! I've never seen that before.

You must hurry: there's no time...

So you've noticed it too? ...I've never seen my pendulum oscillate so fast... Never in my life!

It's incredible... Look! It's absolutely incredible... I've never seen anything like it!

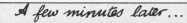

A few minutes later...

This is an ideal place for you to hide. Be sure you don't make any noise. Keep a sharp eye on the prisoners. If all goes well, we'll come straight back here.

Goodbye, Tintin. Goodbye, and good luck!

Good luck to you, Skut.

Why did I ever leave Marlinspike?

Let anyone mention travel to me again and I'll tell him...

CRCCH

?

CAPTAIN?...

CAPTAIN?...

WHERE ARE YOU?!

Billions of blistering barnacles! W-where are you?

Here!

How on earth did you get in there?

I don't know. I went to step over some roots and whoosh! I shot down between them.

I fell on a sort of smooth slab... like a flagstone. Let's investigate. There's something funny about this place...a weird atmosphere.

I can feel it too... But we must push on. We'll look later, if we get time.

Not so fast, Snowy.

Oh! Come and look...quietly...

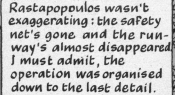

Rastapopoulos wasn't exaggerating: the safety net's gone and the runway's almost disappeared. I must admit, the operation was organised down to the last detail.

I didn't see the plane: must have been camouflaged.

I expect so.

We must be getting near: look at Snowy. He's on to something.

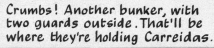

Crumbs! Another bunker, with two guards outside. That'll be where they're holding Carreidas.

Th-th-there!...He...he...he's w-w-waking up... He...he...he...he'll t-t-t-...he'll t-t-talk.

They aren't paying much attention. All the better for us.

Kita di rumah biassa tambah sedikit sambal ulek.

Itu bukan djelek, tentu lebih enak tetapi...

Ssh-h-h-h!... Or bang-bang... Understand?

Understand? Quiet, or else...

Disarm them first, Captain ...Good... Now, tie them up, quick as you can. Better gag them too. You can use their own shirts.

Sorry, old man, but you know now a sailor has a passion for knots!

Now, you moth-eaten monkey, how's that, eh?

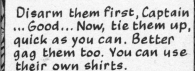

Have you decided? Will you co-operate, or do I use stronger measures? Are you going to talk, you little reptile?

A little reptile... that's what I am. It can't be said too often. There's no excuse, either. Think of all the good examples I had when I was a boy. My grandfather, for instance. Think of my grandfather...

... my maternal grandfather... just a humble confectioner, a maker of Turkish delight in Erzerum. A simple, honest man. "Laszlo", he used to say, "Laszlo, remember: an ill-gotten camel gathers no gain..."

It's all your fault, charlatan! You'll pay for this!

YEOW

Clumsy quack!... You jabbed me with your needle, curse you!

I ... I'm t-terribly sorry ...

The ... the syringe ... it ... it was empty? Doctor! It was empty, wasn't it? ... Tell me!

I ... er ... y-y-yes ...

... it was ... er ... empty ... er ... al-most ... You ... you aren't feeling bad ...

Me? Bad? ... Bad? Me? ... Bad?

Me? Bad? Of course I'm bad! I'm the devil incarnate ... that's what I am. And let's hear anyone try to deny it!

I beg your pardon! I am the devil incarnate ... and I'm richer than you are, too!

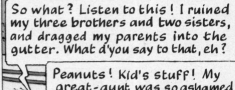
So what? Listen to this! I ruined my three brothers and two sisters, and dragged my parents into the gutter. What d'you say to that, eh?

Peanuts! Kid's stuff! My great-aunt was so ashamed of me she lay down and died! Beat that!

Amateur! You're not in my class. Think of my scheme to kidnap you ... that took a man of real cunning, a man without a shred of decency ... a fiend!

You, doctor. I promised you forty thousand dollars to help me get the account number out of Carreidas. And all the time I'd made a plan to eliminate you when the job was done ... Diabolical, wasn't it? ... Don't you agree?

And the Sondonesian nationalists ... poor deluded fools. I lured them into this. I said I'd help them in their fight for independence. Ha! ha! ha! If only they knew what lies in store for them!

Their junks are mined already. They'll be blown sky-high, long before they see their homeland.

He's a monster!

The same goes for the others ... Spalding, and the aircrew. Rich men, that's what they think they'll be, with the money I flashed under their noses. But they'll be disposed of when I'm ready. Ha! ha! ha! The Devil himself couldn't do better!

Pooh! You aren't out of the nursery!

Now let's get this straight. Yes or no! Do you or do you not admit that I'm wickeder than you?

Never! ... Never, d'you hear? ... I'd sooner die!

All right, if that's what you want! Die!

Quick! Time we intervened!

If you set yourself up as the devil incarnate, my good sir, you answer back. You shut people's mouths...You...

MBLLL

For goodness sake, Mr. Carreidas, we're in danger...

Who gave you permission to interrupt me, pipsqueak? ...Get this into your head: nothing, and nobody, stops Laszlo Carreidas from speaking!

Is that so?!

MBLL MMBBB MMBLL BBMLBBLL

Nothing, and nobody, eh?

Ah, his hat. Thanks, Snowy. Perhaps that'll help restore his temper...

If you'd only be reasonable we shouldn't have to do this, Mr. Carreidas.

MBLLL

We've wasted enough time. Let's go. I'll see if the coast's clear.

Yes, yes, do that. I'm coming.

O.K. No one about. You can bring them.

Coming... coming...

Captain! Captain! Do hurry up!

I'm coming... coming...

Coming, coming! When are you coming? Now, or next week?

I'm sorry...I...I had a spot of bother with some sticking plaster. You know what I mean. I managed to get rid of it in the end...

Good. But hurry now.

We must leave the two Sondonesians. We'll have our hands full with those three comedians. So, off we go!

Right!

Let's hope we don't run into any more trouble.

?

?

BANG

WHIUIUIUW

RATATATATAT

Stop! Don't waste our ammunition. I'm afraid we're going to need it soon enough!

Bandit!

We'll have the whole gang on our backs in less than ten minutes. Quick, we must rejoin the others.

O.K., I'm with you.

MMBLLL

BLMMBL

What... what's going on?... Where am I... What's happened?

What am I doing, bound and gagged? ...Who dared...I... Diavolo! I've been taken prisoner!

WHEEEET   WHEEEET

Blasts on a whistle. That'll be Allan summoning his men. They're on our trail.

Allan's after them. We aren't finished yet...

Faster, Captain, faster...

I must delay them... That shouldn't be too difficult...

! !

He went down like a ninepin. Crumbs! He's passed out.

Thundering typhoons!

What shall we do, Captain? We can't leave him: he's too valuable as a hostage.

I know...

But if we have to carry him they'll catch us up in no time.

Wait... maybe there's another solution.

Just what I'm looking for.

What are you doing?

SNAP

?

I only want to make sure he really is unconscious.

What, with that thorn?

?????...

NNNN!

You see? A well-chosen spot... one little prick, and... whoops-a-daisy!

We must be close to where we left the others...

CRACK

?

What on earth's that?

A monitor!

What's it doing here, pestilential pachyderm?... Looks as if it escaped from the Ice Age!

MMMMMMM
MMMMMMM
MMM   MM

MMMMMMMM

MMBBL
MMMMM
?

I'll catch Carreidas. The Captain will soon pick up Rasta-popoulos.

Foiled! He's after me already!

You won't get far, my beauty!

Where's Rastapopoulos?

Don't know...pfpf ...My gun...pfpf... got hooked up... pfpf...dratted tree ...Terribly sorry...

Not your fault, Captain. A pity, all the same... Still, let's move on. No use chasing after him: he'll be miles away by now.

About ten yards...pfpf... at the most...pfpf... idiots!

All right, Tintin. Let me just collect my gun.

?

Cunning devil...he's escaped!

MBLLL

GRRRR

I left Snowy to guard Carreidas, but I think Kroll-spell would do it just as well.

Hmm.

Quiet!... Ssh!... Listen!... They can't be far...

36

!?!!

HEY! BOSS!

? Allan!... Saved!

BOING

Meanwhile...

I'm not too happy about Krollspell... I think you trust him too far.

I agree it's risky...

BLMMBM... MBMMBL...

...but he knows now that his worthy employer had him booked for a sticky end. So the doctor's as keen as we are to keep out of his clutches. You saw how he helped us?

Yes...I know...but...

YEEEK!

!

W-what a horrible shriek ...It's...bloodcurdling...

Ugh! Enough to make your hair stand on end...

YOWK!

Cheer up, boss: that's the last.

YEOW!

I wonder... It sounded like Rastapopoulos...

Whoever it is, he isn't very happy.

What are you hanging around for? Get after them! And don't forget, I want Carreidas and Krollspell alive! Just...

...crack 'em on the nut, eh?

Idiot!... Must you keep reminding me?!

Follow me, boys!... Death to the enemies of the Sondonesian revolution!

There!...Careful!...Don't make any noise...They mustn't...

Wooah! wooah! wooah! wooah!

!

There they are! I can see them... You press on with the others, Captain.

But I...

Go, Captain! I won't take any chances.

Wooah! Wooah!

BANG

BANG

WHIUUUW

WHIUUUW

O.K. My turn now!...A burst on the left...

RATATATAT

And another on the right.

RATATATAT

Now beat it fast while they think I'm still there...

W-what's the m-matter... I feel... I feel as if someone's speaking right inside my head...

Higher up? To the left? Under a big flat rock...Yes... yes, I'll do as you say...

Now it's my turn to cover you...

No, come with me! I know where we shall be safe!

Safe?... Safe where?... What d'you mean?

I don't know. But there should be a big flat rock higher up. Keep close! This way, quick!

A big flat rock? How on earth can you know that?

Come on! Quick! Hurry!

There!... That's it... Now, behind those bushes...

!   !

38

In you go, doctor. Be careful, there should be about ten steps...

But how do you know?

Yes, I see them.

All right?... Good. Here's Carreidas. Hold him tight in case he falls.

MBLLL

You next, Captain. Quickly! We mustn't let them see where we've gone... Do hurry!

Tintin, I insist! Tell me where you're taking us!

I don't know. But I'm sure it's our only chance. For goodness sake make up your mind!

All right, I'll come.

?

!

Ugghh!...Beastly things! ... Go away!

Oh, come on, Captain! They're quite harmless. They won't eat you.

For heaven's sake come along, Captain!

And be dive-bombed by vampires?... Never! I'm staying here!

BANG

BANG

WHIIIT

!

WHIIIT

BANG

WHIIIT

Ha! ha! Too clever by half! They're cornered!

Tintin!...This is Allan... Come on out! You'd better be sensible, or I might get impatient... and toss a grenade in after you.

No answer?... O.K., if that's how you want it...

 Wait while I take the pin out...

 ...and here she comes...One...two...

 ...thr... ??!?

 I'm crazy! What am I doing? The boss said he wanted Carreidas and the doctor alive!...He'd have my hide for this...

 B-but w-what shall I do with th- this...

 Hey! Take cover, you lot! I'm going to throw this grenade as far as I can.

 Whew! That really had me sweating!

 BOOM

 There, that's got me out of trouble...

What misbegotten madman had that brilliant idea?!... Chucking grenades about!!

 So it was you, clodhopper! Dim-witted oaf! Numbskull!

 Village idiot! What about our prisoners, eh? Where are they?

 Th-th-there... In the c-c-cave...

 Th-th-there...In the c-c-cave! In the c-c-cave! And what's stopping you from getting them out of the c-c-cave; eh?... What are you waiting for!

 Well! Get on with it!... What's stopping you from getting them out, eh?... What are you waiting for?

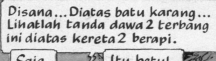

The crew won't be long... then we'll soon crack this... er... sorry, boss... er, have a cigarette?

Shut up!

CRACK

What is that?...

Oh! A monkey!... A prob... a... Got it! A proboscis monkey!

Ha! ha! Look, scooting along like a rabbit!

My, what a sight!... What a conk!... Did ever you see such a conk?

Reminds me of someone... Now, who can it...

Meanwhile...

Hello! Here's one of our chaps come back...

Big man 'e want you: make you go, chop chop...

Now what's the matter?

It should have been finished hours ago, and the plane at the bottom of the sea. We shall end up being spotted here. Ah, here's the news bulletin.

There is still no trace of the aircraft owned by millionaire Laszlo Carreidas which disappeared between Macassar and Darwin. The search, which has been called off at nightfall, will be resumed at dawn.

Good, that gives us a few hours' respite. Come on, boys.

Not me! I'm not crawling about in the jungle...

That'll do, Spalding. Move!

Look here, Tintin, when are you going to explain? Where the blue blistering blazes are you taking us?

I've told you, Captain, I haven't the remotest idea... Someone seems to be guiding me. I'm just obeying orders. That's all I can say...

And another thing: how is it we can see our way down here? By rights it should be black as the inside of a cow.

I know. It's queer. It reminds me of that strange light in the Temple of the Sun.

But I think we've nearly reached our destination... Yes, there's the statue I was told about...

His lordship's "voices" have described the statue to his lordship, of course. Perhaps they've also been gracious enough to explain why it's so hellishly hot down here! Like a Turkish bath!

I don't know. Perhaps there's a spring of boiling water nearby...

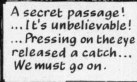

Maybe they serve cups of tea, too!

It could be lava. We are very close to a volcano. Excuse me...

The eye... Press hard on the eye... The right one?... I see...

A secret passage! ...It's unbelievable! ...Pressing on the eye released a catch... We must go on.

In there? But...

I'll come last, Captain. You go, then I can lower the statue into place.

CRACK

I bolted it behind us as I was told to do: I believe we're safe now, if I've really understood the instructions from what you call my "voices".

Your voices!

MMBL

Voices here! Voices there! I suppose you think you're Joan of Arc, eh? I've had enough of this tomfoolery. Thundering typhoons, the joke's over! Tell me how you knew this place existed. Billions of bilious blue blistering barnacles, tell me!

But I ...

MMBL

W-w-what?...
W-w-who?...W-
who's speaking?
...What did you say?
...I...I'm not to make
so much noise?..N-n-
no, sir.

I... It's crazy!...I...You can't imagine what... It's...it's as though someone was talking on the telephone, ringing me up inside my head!...You can laugh, but that's what happened, just like I said...

TAP TAP TAP

Ssh!...
Listen!

TAP TAP

Footsteps!

Yes.

TAP TAP TAP

Someone there!

!

D'you understand? It was just like a loudspeaker, inside my head!...I can't believe it...It's absolutely...

Fan-tas-tic!

Calculus!

Professor!...Where have you come from?...And where are the others?

You see! I was quite right, wasn't I?

You still don't believe me? You're still sceptical?

No, no, Professor, but ...

Oh?...Well, it's perfectly simple: you can ask that gentleman there...

Good evenink, gentlemen. Happy meetink you here.

Name is Mik Kanrokitoff. Have been guidink you.

The famous Kanrokitoff, of the magazine 'Space-Week'?

Guidink?

Certainly. You see tiny instrument with mini-aerial?

Yes, what's that little whisker for?

Thought transmitter... Telepathy is phenomenon attractink very little study in world of science... human world of science, zat is. In other world of science, thought transmission has been common for many years.

Other world? What other world?

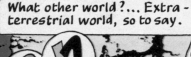

What other world?... Extra-terrestrial world, so to say.

You aren't trying to make us believe that you...

Me?... Niet!... Ordinary human beink like you.

I am initiate, so to say... Zat is, like number of other men, actink as link between earth and... another planet. My job to keep...er... extra-terrestrials informed on all aspects of human activity... Understand-ink?... Meetink with zem on zis island, twice a year...

...in zis ancient temple forgotten by men, but not by...er... others, who have been comink here for thousands of years... You saw statue? Astronaut, yes?

I've had enough of you and your cock-and-bull story! I don't believe a word of it. You can't fool me with your astro-nomical asininities!

I...Yes, sir.., No, sir... I won't speak again...I beg your pardon? ... No, I won't interrupt...

Nu, to continue. Astroship bring-ink me here last night. Zis morn-ink observed great activity on zis island, which is usually deserted. Am watchink extra-ordinary preparations, zen aeroplane is landink. Have realised zat operation is trap...

AAAAH

45

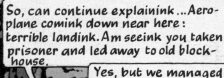
So, can continue explainink ...Aeroplane comink down near here: terrible landink. Am seeink you taken prisoner and led away to old blockhouse.

Yes, but we managed to escape...

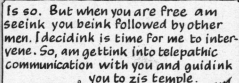
Is so. But when you are free am seeink you beink followed by other men. I decidink is time for me to intervene. So, am gettink into telepathic communication with you and guidink you to zis temple.

You saved our lives! Without your help, who knows...

TCHOOO

?

OH?

AH!

Have you lost something?

Can't you see my hat has fallen off?

?

Some people need every single thing spelled out in words of one syllable.

Now extra-terrestrials must be decidink what to do with you. Am expectink astroship very soon...You in your world say flyink-saucer.

A flying-saucer?!

So now we've come to flying-saucers! You're going too far: we aren't as gullible as that!

You still doubt? So, look over there, to your right.

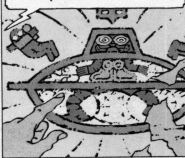
See there, on wall. Is certainly machine used by people from...er... other planet.

Thousands of years ago, men were buildink zis temple to worship gods who are comink from sky in fire-chariots. In fact, fire-chariots are astroships, like zat one. And gods... but you have seen statue: what are you thinkink statue is resemblink?

It looks...it looks like an astronaut with a helmet, microphone, earphones...

And there, on the left, down by the statue...What's that?

?

A HAT! IT'S CARREIDAS'S HAT!

You're sure it's his? See if it has his initials.

?

Confounded thing, it won't come out... It's jammed under the pedestal.

If it slipped under the statue you must be able to get it out, fool!... It hasn't been glued to the floor! Pull, you milksop, Pull hard! Pull!...

HNN!... HNN!...

RRCH!

IMBECILE! IMBECILE! IMBECILE!

Sorry, boss! So sorry!

L.C.: Laszlo Carreidas... It's his all right. Look, boss.

So... you had to rip the brim to pull it free?

That means the statue was standing on it... In which case... Of course, it's obvious: there must be a secret passage... So start looking! All of you!

Go on! Go on! The statue must be hinged...

Ten minutes later...

It won't shift, boss... If only we had some dynamite.

Dynamite?... We can do better than that!

Quick, go back to our junk and bring all the plastic explosive intended for those silly Sondonesians! Hurry!

Aha, my clever friends, you don't know Rastapopoulos... I'll get you, if I have to demolish this temple stone by stone!

Meanwhile...

That fool Allan! What's he doing now?...

He should have been back ages ago. I'll blow their statues sky-high...Then we'll see... Hello?

?

The bump on my head...it's gone!...That's a good omen: it means my luck's changing!

BROMM

? ? ?

AN EARTHQUAKE!

What have I done to deserve all this? Me, who'd never harm a fly!...There's no justice!

At the same time...

WOO-OOO-AAH

Yes, is over... Earthquakes very frequent in zis area, but never severe...Yet zis time am wonderink...

This time?...

Cuthbert, please!

I beg your pardon: he started it!

Your hat? You have it on your head.

I not know why, but zis time I feelink very very uneasy...

Oh?

Yes, am sensink somethink strange in air. Must not stay here... Come, will rejoin your comrades.

What's been going on?

No, it was him!

Come quickly. Have warnink of danger.

50

Zis gallery is runnink from temple at one end to crater of extinct volcano at other.

BOOMM

Look here, how many more earthquakes have you got up your sleeve?

Zat was not earthquake. Is somethink else: probably explosion set off by zose gangsters. We must hurry. I sensink great danger very close.

Few more minutes and we are comink out of underground...

...the main thing is, I found my hat.

Of course.

?

PLOP

Good heavens, it's dripping on my head... In that case, what am I wearing?

Wait for me. I won't be a minute. I must find my hat!

!

It's on your head! ... Come back!

Yes, yes! Your hat's on your head, Mr. Carreidas.

No, this one isn't mine! It leaks!

!

Crumbs! Those trails of smoke ...Where are they coming from?

And what's that awful smell?... It's sulphur!

AAAH

?

Well done, Captain! A brilliant recovery!

Let yourself slide down now...

This way, Captain!

Phew! I thought I was in the frying-pan that time!

Come on quickly! We haven't a moment to lose!

I'm coming, I'm coming. That ectoplasm Carreidas, he'd better watch out! Purple profiteering jellyfish! He'll be steak and kidney pudding if I catch him!

Hurry!

It's like a furnace down here now.

Ah, is good, is good! You safe and sound! Come zis way!

The volcano's come to life.

Alas so. Earthquake probably caused small crack in old feed pipe of volcano. Is not so dangerous. But zen explosion is set off...

...and is enlargink crack and allowink gas and lava to escape...In zat case, eruption of volcano is followink...Let us be hopink astroship is comink at rendezvous...

The heat is becoming intolerable ... If this goes on...

ATCHOO

Shut the door behind you! Can't you feel the draught? Dreadful!

⁉⁈!

And what about all this smoke? You're doing it on purpose. Me with my sensitive throat! Are you trying to kill me?

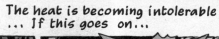
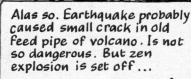

Now is comink poisonous gas! Hold handkerchiefs over your mouths!

Come on, keep moving!

Well, well, well? What's happening now?

Let's see, what's this down here?

Zis way, quickly! We are nearly outside...

Come on, come on. And hold that over your nose!

Phew! At last! A lovely breath of good fresh air.

Astroship should be comink here, to old crater.

Look over there! The sky's blood red!

Yes, yes, must be lava flowink down side of volcano...

Wait! Wait for me! Allan! Allan! Help! Not so fast! Wait for me!

Ve...rubber...dinghy! ...It'f our only... meanf... of efcape!

Have we got everyone?

Er... I think so... yes...

Cuthbert!!... Where is Cuthbert???

The professor! He must have been left behind!

WOOAH! WOOAAH!

Tintin!... Come back, for heaven's sake!... Come back, Tintin!

WOOAAAOOAAAH

He's gone into that inferno!... Call him back!... Do something!... I don't know... ring him up... telepathise him!

WOOWOWOWOON

Come back, my young comrade. Is useless risk-ink your life.

?

What happened? Did he answer?

Yes, is answerink ...Is tellink me to go to...! And such polite boy, I thinkink!

Help me!...Here... help me!

He's back!

!

Blistering barnacles! Good old Tintin! He's got him!

Quick...the kiss of life...We must ...revive him ...

Hip hip hooray! They're safe!

Yippee! Who's coming for a midnight bathe?

Here, Snowy. Not too far.

Pooh, I can swim, can't I?

Still no sign of astroship... Why are zey so late?

How's that, Cuthbert?...Better?

Oooh

Look! Look! Water! Lake is emptyink like sink!

WOOAAH!

RRHOORR RHOR

!

WOOABLUBBLUB

Coming, Snowy!...Hang on!

Wooah
Wooah

Another few seconds and the lake
will have vanished!...Whatever...

RRHOR

BAOUM

How long must
I put up with
all this dust?

Whew! That's that for
the time being! Lucky
it was only ash and
water vapour, not lava
and chunks of rock!

BZZ BZZ BZZ

Astroship! Astroship!
...Is zere...right above
us... Can hear it!

What, that
buzzing
like a bee?

BZZ BZZZ BZZ BZZZ

Not a
thing
to be
seen...

I take my hat
off to them if
they land in this
murky gloom!

A balloon?
...Here?...
Impossible!!

Yes, please be hurryink:
zere could be another
eruption... Yes, be
lowerink ladder,
please...

You are goink aboard
astroship. But first, as
am explainink, I hypnotise
you.

57

Hypnotise us? Not on your life! It's out of the question ... Besides, that sort of mummery wouldn't affect us!

Wouldn't affect us ... wouldn't affect us ... wouldn't affect us wouldn't ...

Now, gentlemen, you are at airport at Djakarta. You are boardink Carreidas aircraft, flyink to Sydney. Zere is ladder. Please go up first, Mr. Carreidas.

You followink him, professor, and zen you, Captain Skut.

Gino, please ... Now you go up, doctor.

You takink Snowy, Tintin ... And last is goink Captain Haddock.

Excellent ... You are all in aircraft ...

You raisink ladder quickly, Chief Pilot! I hearink dangerous rumblinks ...

Is just in time! ... Thankink you, Chief Pilot. You excusink me now while I lookink after terrestrial comrades.

You, Mr. Carreidas. You playink Battleships with Captain Haddock. You cheatink, naturally.

Naturally.

Captain Skut, you are at controls of Carreidas 160. Flight is uneventful. Nothink to report.

Nothink to report. No, nothink at all!

Look zere! ... Rubber dinghy!

Is dinghy from Carreidas 160 ... Zat is suggestink how adventure can be finishink for Tintin and comrades.

I fee fomefing in ve fky! What if it?

It's ... it's a flying-saucer!! It's circling ... Diavolo! It's coming straight for us! Fire, Allan! ... FIRE!

58

You puttink guns down, criminals!... Game is up!...You are in my hypnotic power.

All listenink carefully. Zis machine is simply helicopter comink to pick you up... You climbink aboard!

Yes, sir. Yes, sir.

Now I speakink to you, Captain Skut, and to your comrades... You are forgetting everythink zat is happenink since yester-day. You only rememberink zis: after departure from Djakarta for Sydney, unknown causes are forcink you to be ditchink aircraft...

... and you are havink to board rubber dinghy.

All in boat?...Skut, Calculus, Gino, Carreidas, Haddock, Tintin, Snowy. Good ... I takink charge of others ... Now sleep, comrades. Zat is my command!

Adieu!

Wooah! Wooah!

Some hours later...

Search has been resumed for the passengers and crew of the Carreidas aircraft which disappeared yesterday on a flight to Sydney. Hopes are fading of finding survivors, but aircraft ...

..continue to patrol the area. During the night a volcano thought to be extinct has erupted on the island of Pulau-pulau Bompa in the Celebes Sea. A column of smoke more than thirty thousand feet high is rising from the crater. Observers are keeping watch on the volcano and are studying the eruption from the air.

One more run, Dick. See if we can film the crater.

O.K.

Hey, Dick! Look down there, at ten o'clock. Look!

Good Lord! A rubber dinghy!

Victor Hotel Bravo calling Macassar tower. We've spotted a rubber dinghy about a mile south of the volcano. Five or six men aboard. We've made several low-level runs over them but there's no sign of life...except for a little white dog.

Look, Dick! The wind's carrying them towards the island, and there's lava flowing into the sea. They'll be boiled alive like lobsters! We've got to do something. We must save them!

Wooah! Wooah!

Thousands of miles away, several days later.

Tonight Scanorama is bringing you a special feature. The brilliant air-sea rescue of six of the men aboard millionaire Carreidas's plane made world headline news. Laszlo Carreidas and five companions were found drifting in a dinghy more than 200 miles off their scheduled route. They were snatched to safety only minutes from death in a lava-heated cauldron, the sea around the volcanic island of Pulau-pulau Bompa. All the survivors were suffering from severe shock. It was several hours before they...

...recovered consciousness in a Javanese hospital. Our on-the-spot reporter has secured the first interview with the mystery-crash survivors...Colin Chattamore in Djakarta.

A put-up job, or I'm not Jolyon Wagg! Bet Carreidas dumped his rotten old crate for the insurance.

Let's begin with the owner of the aircraft... This has been a terrible business for you, Mr.Carreidas. You must be greatly upset by the loss of your prototype, and the tragic disappearance of your secretary and two members of your crew.

Yes, of course ...

All very sad, but what can you expect? That's life, you know. What really annoys me, though, is that I lost my hat: a pre-war Bross and Clackwell. And that's absolutely irreplaceable.

About the needle-marks found on your arm, Mr.Carreidas. It seems that your companions didn't have these...

Naturally: I'm richer than they are.

I...er...precisely.

Captain Skut, you had to make a forced landing. Can you tell us something about it, and what happened afterwards? Your last radio message said you were flying over Sumbawa and had nothing to report.

Yes...

...yes, but is not possible to remember: is like gap in my mind... I not understand ... Is like strange dream...

Me too. Just the same. Only I'd call it a horrible nightmare.

Blow me! Look who's here again. My old chum! The ancient mariner from Marlinspike!...The old humbug, he doesn't half come up with some comic turns!

I vaguely remember some grinning masks, and suffocating heat in an underground passage... Thundering typhoons, it makes me thirsty to think of it!

And how about you?

I...well, I had a similar dream. It's certainly odd, but...

And there's his pal, young Sherlock Holmes!

... the most inexplicable part of this whole business is...No, I think Professor Calculus will tell you ...

Would you agree with the photographer, who claims that it is indeed a flying-saucer?... And would you say that this machine is of extra-terrestrial origin?

A bottle of gin?... Frankly, I can see no connection... To me, the photograph would appear to show an unidentified flying object, popularly known as a flying-saucer.

Do you think this 'machine' is connected with the object you found?

Round? That goes without saying. A saucer is always round, is it not?

Er...of course... One final question, Professor. I understand that you and your companions are suffering from amnesia...

If you wish, but I always take a glass of water with milk of magnesia.

I beg your pardon?...I...hmm...the point I want to make is that occasional cases of amnesia are not uncommon... There's one reported in the paper today. The head of a psychiatric clinic in Cairo, Dr. Krollspell, has just been found wandering near the outskirts of the city. He'd been missing for more than a month, and he has completely lost his memory.

But in your case, how do the doctors account for the fact that you are ALL suffering from amnesia?

They don't seem able to give an explanation ... any more than we can.

I could tell them a thing or two!... But no one would believe me!

And finally, what are your plans? Where do you go from here?

We're catching the next plane for Sydney. We shall just be in time for the opening of the Astronautical Congress.

Well, I hope there will be no further interruptions to your journey. Good luck from Scanorama, and thank you ... Goodbye, Captain!

Goodbye!

DONG. This is the final call for Qantas Flight 714 to Sydney. All passengers please proceed immediately to gate No. 3.

THE END

62